children's choice®

this book belongs
to

_____

mary alice

OPERATOR NUMBER 9

Story by Jeffrey Allen
Pictures by James Marshall

Little, Brown and Company

BOSTON   TORONTO

A Children's Choice® Book Club Edition From Scholastic Book Services

FOR MY PARENTS
J.A.

FOR ARNOLD LOBEL
J. M.

Mrs. Johnson wanted to set her watch, so she dialed the
time service and listened carefully to the operator.
"At the sound of the tone, the time will be eight-fifteen
and ten seconds, exactly. Quack!"
Mrs. Johnson hung up the receiver and set her watch.
Who could that nice operator be? she wondered.

It was Mary Alice, Operator Number Nine.
All day long Mary Alice told people the correct time.
"At the sound of the tone, the time will be eight-sixteen,
exactly. Quack!"

Everyone in town had faith in Mary Alice.
"She's so efficient and responsible," people would say.

Mary Alice, Operator Number Nine, loved her job.
She never got tired, and she never made mistakes.

But one day something terrible happened. Mary Alice's throat felt sore and scratchy. Her nose was runny. And her chest was all wheezy.

"I think I have a cold," she told Boss Chicken.

Boss Chicken told Mary Alice to go straight home.

Mary Alice felt bad about leaving her job.
"Don't worry," clucked Boss Chicken. "I'll find someone
to take your place until you're better. It's an easy job."
Mary Alice felt even worse.

She went straight home and gargled with warm salt-water.

"Who is going to take my place?" she asked herself.

At the telephone company, many people came to apply for Mary Alice's position.

"One at a time," clucked the Boss.

Eric Snake was first to try.

"Oh goody," hissed Eric. "I've always wanted a job like this."
But Eric was not right for the time service.
He had such a sinister little voice.

"At the sound of the tone, it will be ten-twenty, exactly.
Hisssssssss."
People were frightened when they heard Eric's voice.
"This isn't the job for you, Eric," said the Boss.

"Why not give *me* a chance?" asked Jake Dog.
"Very well," said the Boss.
Jake Dog did his best, but he didn't know how to be
precise.

"At the sound of the tone, it will be sometime in the morning, around eleven, I should think. Woof!"
But people leaving on trips needed to know the exact time, and Jake Dog wasn't giving it.

At home in bed Mary Alice was a bundle of nerves. She was worrying about her job.

Maybe the new person will be so good that Boss Chicken won't want me back, she thought.

When she could stand the suspense no longer, Mary Alice gave Boss Chicken a call.

"Everything is just dandy," said the Boss. "Don't worry about a thing."

And she hung up quickly.

Mary Alice didn't feel better at all.

"You're next," said Boss Chicken to Charlie Armadillo.

"Splendid," said Charlie, adjusting his spectacles.
"Where is the clock?"
"Right in front of you," said the Boss.
Charlie's eyesight was not the best, and he was always
making mistakes.

"At the sound of the tone, it will be, now let me see, ten forty-five, or is that nine o'clock? I can't be sure."
But athletes needed to know the right time too, and Charlie was no help at all.

Connie Hyena tried out next. "This is going to be fun,"
she said.
But Connie had a problem.
Connie was a laugher.

"At the sound of — ha ha ha ha ha — the tone, it will —
hee hee hee, ho ho ho, har har har."
People found Connie's laughter annoying.

All over town people were talking about the changes in time service.

"It's not like it used to be," they sighed. "What ever happened to that efficient Mary Alice, Operator Number Nine?"

"I'd like to give it a try," said May Beaver.
"You might as well," said the Boss, who was running out
of patience.
"I'm sure I'll be very good," said May.

But May was too eager. She couldn't wait for people to
call, so she called them — often at the most inappropri-
ate times.

"Forget it, May," said the Boss.

Now there was no one left, and Boss Chicken was beside herself. She jumped up and down and plucked at her feathers.

"It's up to me," she vowed. "Boss Chicken will take Mary Alice's place!"

She put on a set of headphones and answered the next call.

"At the sound of the tone it will be twelve-ten exactly. Cluck!"

"That's incorrect!" said a familiar voice at the other end of the line.

"It's twelve-eleven."

Boss Chicken was ashamed. "Thank you, Mary Alice," she said.

When Mary Alice came back to work after her cold was over, she found a present waiting for her. It was a box of candy and a new set of headphones. Inside was a note:

Dear Mary Alice,
      No one can do the job the way you do, not even me. Welcome back to work.
                              Signed,
              Nancy Chicken, your grateful boss

Mary Alice smiled and took the next call.

The Children's Choice® Clubhouse

It's the perfect place for playing or for curling up with a good book ★ Big enough to hold a few friends (it's 3' x 4½' and 4½' tall) ★ Made of sturdy corrugated cardboard with a washable finish ★ Decorated inside and out with whimsical illustrations in full color ★ A very special gift.

To order, please send your name and address with a check or money order for $19.95 to:

Children's Choice® Clubhouse
Scholastic Inc.
900 Sylvan Ave.
Englewood Cliffs
New Jersey 07632